You Can't Catch Me
ANNABEL COLLIS

RED FOX

For Emma and Oliver

A Red Fox Book

Published by Random House Children's Books
20 Vauxhall Bridge Road, London SW1V 2SA

A division of Random House UK Ltd
London Melbourne Sydney Auckland
Johannesburg and agencies throughout the world

Copyright © Annabel Collis 1993
Designed by Rowan Seymour

1 3 5 7 9 10 8 6 4 2

First published in Great Britain by The Bodley Head 1993

Red Fox edition 1994

Printed in China

RANDOM HOUSE UK Limited Reg. No. 954009

ISBN 0 09 932101 7

ADVENTURE PLAYGROUND

'The adventure playground's this way. Stay close Oliver. Hold tight and don't get lost.'
'Well I would stay close, but…

Monkey and me
want a real adventure . . .

on a ship that sails
on a stormy sea.

And you can't catch me.

And I'm not scared,
and I won't fall

in the raging river where the
great big crocodiles

SNAP their teeth,

and the hungry hippos
snoozy sleep.

Help! The water's deep.

Quick, pull me up
to the island safe,

in the jungle green,

where the animals chase.

But they can't catch me.

We're sliding fast
down a tunnel dark,

only room for four,
there's no room for more.

We're glad to be back,
my monkey and me,

and we're ready for tea. '